NED and the WORLD'S RELIGIONS

as seen through the eyes of children

by
Ron Madison

Illustrations by
David Covolo

My purpose in writing this book . . .

is to present a glimpse of the world's major religions through the eyes of children, capturing their ease of feeling and thought…their youthful exuberance, their joy. Each story is a vignette, a brief visit, a shared moment. From these stories I have learned that a child's religious belief can be a great gift, a driving influence to love all humanity and to understand the true meaning of …

"Do unto others as you would have them do unto you."

Ron Madison

www.nedsheadbooks.com

About the cover art:

The symbols on the cover, arranged in no particular order by the artist, represent from left to right:

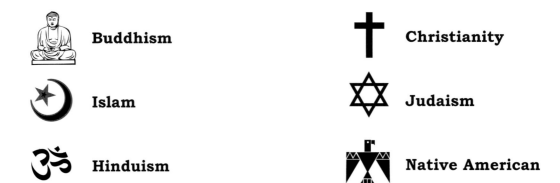

Buddhism   **Christianity**

Islam   **Judaism**

Hinduism   **Native American**

ISBN 10: 1-887206-26-4   Printed in the U. S. A.   First Printing 2008
ISBN 13: 978-1-887-20626-6

Introduction

The following is from a letter written to the author by:

Dr. Gerald L. Zahorchak
Secretary of Education
Commonwealth of Pennsylvania

Dear Ron:

This great and wonderful country was founded on the ideals of freedom, especially religious freedom. As Secretary of Education in Pennsylvania [one of the nation's most populated and diverse states], I have learned to understand that simple yet complex thought, and I appreciate the opportunity it has given me…to live and work in a country where individuals' voices matter and where we respect each other's differences, where all the major religions live peacefully side-by-side, where "the religion" isn't government and where the government isn't "the religion." In fact, Americans may be the best example of how well diverse populations not only tolerate others' differences but actually work together on behalf of everyone and especially those who are least among us.

In America, most of us—a large majority—have religious beliefs, and we understand our own religious denominations. But we know little about others' religions. That, in my opinion, is a cause for concern. In this sometimes restless world where religion frequently is the sword of conflict rather than the dove of peace, it is best that our nation, as the global leader, understands the beliefs of others throughout the world. Where better to start that understanding than with our children in our own land?

Further, I believe that our country needs to expect that Americans will learn about the world's religions. Our nation's schools, both in basic and higher education, are the logical place for that learning to occur. This does not mean that some religion's prayer(s) belong in the public school; rather this is about developing religious literacy. Articles about basic and higher education have called for improving religious literacy via course offerings that would respect the necessity of separating religious study from religious practice. We really should begin this religious study as part of civics education—its time is far past due.

When we become more literate with the world's religions, we can learn:

Virtually all the world's religions value charity, love for others, and the Golden Rule, and all believe in love and respect for something greater than we are.

Most religions organize, or set rules, for their followers, while respecting those who follow another religion. No one needs to win in terms of whose rules are a better way to love; everyone simply needs to love. . .

Dr. Zahorchak went on to explain to the author what he had in mind. He suggested that Dr. Madison use Ned to help young people understand how other young people of different religions feel. The result was this book, which prompted these further remarks by Dr. Zahorchak:

"Ron set about the charge most seriously, as he always does when he prepares to write. He traveled about the country, stayed on Indian reservations, attended various religious services, and experienced various practices firsthand (practices like the Shoshone Sundance, the Jewish Rosh Hashanah, the Tibetan Buddhist Fire Puja, and attended many religious services in various churches, temples and shrines). In the process he has written about the four most populous religions in the world (Christianity, Islam, Hinduism and Buddhism) as well as two that are of particular interest here in America (Judaism and Native American). After two solid years of hands-on research comes *Ned and the World's Religions, as seen through the eyes of children*, another delightful Ned book that comes to America at such an important time.

"This book takes an extremely difficult subject through the filters, or eyes, of young children and makes understanding extraordinarily uncomplicated. I am uplifted by the impressions that have come from combining the children's interpretations and the author's descriptions of his experience with each child. This is a giant step towards understanding and peace.

"Ron's writing is done in poetry. Each story is the result of his interview with a child. Let's begin with the study of and respect for the world's diverse religions.

"We need to understand each other. . . That's a giant step to peace."

Dr. Gerald L. Zahorchak
Secretary of Education
Commonwealth of Pennsylvania

Contents

Prologue

I recently heard an Indian fable:

One evening an old Cherokee told his grandson about a battle that goes on inside people. He said:

"My son, the battle is between two 'wolves' inside us all.

"One is Dark. It is anger, envy, jealousy, regret, greed, arrogance, self-pity, guilt, resentment, inferiority, lies, false pride, superiority, and ego.

"The other is Good. It is joy, peace, love, hope, serenity, humility, kindness, benevolence, empathy, generosity, truth, compassion, and faith."

"The grandson thought about it for a minute and then asked his grandfather, 'Which wolf wins?' "

The old Cherokee simply replied, "The one you *feed*."

We are all tempted from time to time to spend our energy and resourcefulness seeking self-satisfaction and self-aggrandizement. We sway from the common good or what most people think is "right." One word captures the higher road to me – transcendence. The best stories of all religions seem to call us to transcend – to rise above – the callings that would lead us away from the common good.

I believe the essence of this book is an invitation. Each of us is invited to do what Ron Madison did in putting together this book: approach people different from ourselves in a spirit of child-like openness and with a willingness to respectfully listen. His inquisitive spirit, housed in the body of an ol' linebacker-engineer, which Ron was, seems to approach the *Mysterium Tremendum* – with a respect and love for the Divine Mystery and for other people.

Ron offers a gentle invitation for all of us to be the best that we can be: where the great influence of religion is not divisive, but collegial; not judgmental, but cooperative; not dogmatic, but explorative.

It has been a great blessing for me to be a part of Ron's journey. My hope is that this book will inspire everyone who reads it or listens to it, to follow Ned's and Ron's child-like exploration into the lives and values, the very souls of those around us in this ever-expanding and increasingly diverse world of ours. The world is growing smaller. And we, as spiritual beings, need to grow larger. May this book *feed* your spirit and increase your appetite for the good of all.

Rev. Dr. William E. Carpenter
Pastor, Johns Creek Methodist Church
Johns Creek, Georgia

The Soccer Game

Ned was proud of his friends that day.
   They were going to win and go on to play
    for the championship the following week,
    a goal they never expected to reach.

For they had no star, no one was great.
   They played as a team; that was their trait.
   They played for each other, as diverse as they were.
   They won for each other, that's for sure.

When they left the field, happy and proud,
Coach called them together and said aloud:
"Let's all join hands and pray with each other
for the friendships we've gained playing together."

"I won't," said one, as he stopped and pulled back.
"My God is not yours. It's as simple as that."
"Nor is mine," another joined in.
"Nor mine, " said a third. "If I did I would sin."

Coach looked at them and offered this thought:
    "Are we really as different as we've been taught?
    Let's find out. Let's just see.
    Let's tell each other what we believe.

"The next time we meet, what I'd like you to do
    is tell us what you believe to be true."

Lindsey's Story – Christian

Christ and Christmas

It's all about love. What I really believe
    is that Christ lived his life for you and for me.
    That's why he came, why he was born,
    so long ago on Christmas morn.

I do love Christmas. It's such great fun,
    so full of joy for everyone.
    Beautiful songs and presents galore;
    how could anyone ask for more?

But Christmas to me is much, much more.
    It's the birth of a child that I adore.
    He loves me, and I know it's true.
    I can feel his love when I need to.

He died to show us how to live,
    how to love and how to give.
    I know he died for you and me.
    What greater love can there be?

And just who was this holy one?
    I believe he was God's son."

**"In everything, do unto others
as you would have them do to you."**

Jesus, Matthew 7:12

Gazal's Story
Hindu

Yoga

Want to know what I like to do?
    Yoga.   Surprised? It's really true.

It's a neat way to start the day.
    A great way to relax and pray,
    to rid your mind of troubling things,
    to enjoy the peace that quiet brings.

Yoga's very, very old.
    Ancient Hindus, I've been told,
    learned to clear their heart and mind
    of earthly things of every kind.
    For days they'd focus on their goal,
    to be with God within their soul.

Holi, the Festival of Colors

It's my very favorite holiday.
    A time for color and for play.

A time for parades and laughter too.
    You splash me, and I splash you
    with water and powder in colors bright.
    What a wonderful, beautiful fun-filled sight.

Holi is based on a mythical story,
    where a man of good, in all his glory,
    destroyed the evil ruling king,
    destroyed the darkness, brought light in.

It's a day for fun. We're proud and glad
    to bless the triumph of good over the bad."

**"This is the sum of duty: do not do to
others what would cause pain if done to you."**
    Mahabharata, 5:1517

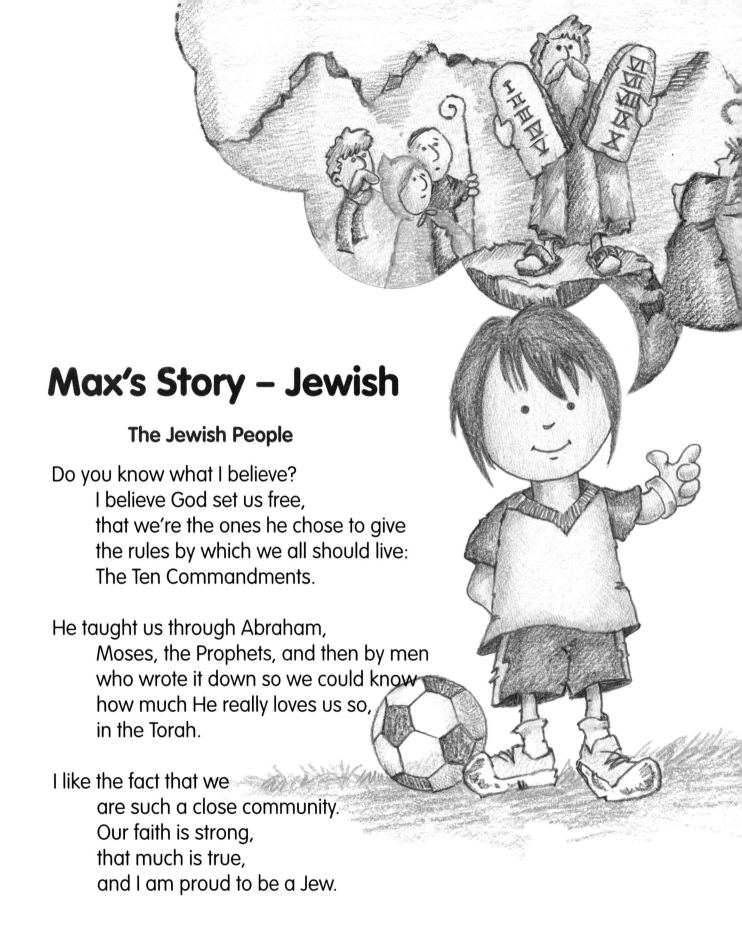

Max's Story – Jewish

The Jewish People

Do you know what I believe?
 I believe God set us free,
 that we're the ones he chose to give
 the rules by which we all should live:
 The Ten Commandments.

He taught us through Abraham,
 Moses, the Prophets, and then by men
 who wrote it down so we could know
 how much He really loves us so,
 in the Torah.

I like the fact that we
 are such a close community.
 Our faith is strong,
 that much is true,
 and I am proud to be a Jew.

Hanukkah

It's a time for us to remember when we regained our temple in Jerusalem.
   We filled it once again with light from a menorah, on that first night.
   But the menorah used oil of a special kind,
   and one night's supply was all they could find.
   To replace the oil took eight days. Yet all that while, the steady rays
   from the first night's light kept the temple bright.
   It was a miracle. Another in God's way
   of blessing the Jews, on that day.

Today it's a wonderful time to gather the family, have fun, and dine.
   My grandmother's latkes, they're the best.
   Best in the world, that's my guess.
   They're my favorite Hanukkah treat,
   and her matzo ball soup can't be beat.

It lasts eight days. Each night we
   light a candle for all to see.
   The first night one, the second, two,
   'til eight are lit, when we are through.
   That's when I get to see
   all the presents for
   sister and me.

**"What is hateful to you, do not do to your fellowman.
This is the entire law; all the rest is commentary."**

Talmud, Shabbat 3id

Ricky's Story – Native American

The Creator and Mother Earth

Grandmother taught me the ancient way,
    the Arapaho songs, and how we pray
    to the great Creator, who made all things.
    Who made Mother Earth and all she brings:

The water we drink, the rivers, the snows,
the mountains and plains, and all that grows,
the elk, the deer, the eagle and crow,
and most of all our buffalo,
whose meat we ate, whose hide we wore.

All of that and much, much more.

That's why it's important to stem our greed.
        To take what she gives, not more than we need.

The Sweat Lodge

And grandmother taught me our special way
        of gathering together just to pray.
        With friends and family, we sat around
        steamy rocks and made not a sound,
        in a beaver-like lodge filled with steam.
        It was dark and cramped, like a bad dream.

As I prayed and sweat, every care and sin
        seemed to ooze from my
        body, and peace came in.

**"All things are our relatives;
what we do to everything,
        we do to ourselves.
        All is really one."**
Black Elk

Karma's Story
Buddhist

The Dalai Lama

It was September when Dalai Lama came.
    A beautiful day, not a sign of rain.
    The entire town appeared that day
    just to hear what he had to say.

He stood there tall, with an awkward grace
    and a kindly smile upon his face.
    And as he spoke, we'd often hear
    his child-like laugh, which made it clear
    he spoke from the heart.

    It was not pride, but love, you see,
    that crafted his words so humbly:

            "When I was very small indeed,
            I had a parrot I'd care for and feed.

            "For that, he accepted me, nothing more.
            It was a monk, my teacher, that he adored.
            He was happy to see the monk come.
            He'd leap and sing and carry on.

"But he was my parrot; didn't he know
it was to me he owed affection? So –
I poked him hard! And then I guess
his love for me was even less.

"Therefore, the point is simply this,
to give without affection is to miss
the whole spirit of giving."

"Like humans, animals know whether affection is genuine or not.
True affection leads to tolerance, forgiveness and happiness."

The Dalai Lama,
Woodstock, NY, September 21, 2006

Karam's Story
Muslim

Muhammad and the Quran

After Moses and Jesus,
Mohammad came,
   the last great
   prophet to speak
   in God's name.

Allah, our God, to Mohammad passed on
   the sacred words of the holy Quran.
   Through Mohammad He spoke in Arabic and rhyme,
   repeating His words from earlier time
   to Moses, the Prophets and Jesus too,
   and pledged to Mohammad His words were true.

Our beliefs are much like the Christian and Jew,
   for indeed they are Allah's people too.

Ramadan and Eid al-Fitr

We honor Allah's gift, the Holy Quran,
    once a year during Ramadan.
    For thirty days we fast and pray
    and practice charity. That way
    our devotion to Allah, our self-sacrifice,
    will help keep us steadfast all our life.

Eid al-Fitr, on Ramadan's last day,
    is a time to be grateful, a time to be gay,
    to decorate our home, to dress up real fine,
    and, after all the fasting, to really dine.
    For kids, this time is especially fun
    'cause that's when all the presents come.

I like to help others, and when my life's gone,
    Allah will know just what I've done.

"Not one of you is a believer until you wish for others that which you wish for yourself."

Number 13 of Imam
"Al-Narawi's Forty Hadiths."

19

Lillian's Story – Christian

The Service

It's not just for adults; it's for everyone.
    And for me it's really lots of fun.
    I like the choir, the songs they sing,
    the rhythm, the dance, the joy it all brings.

Pastor Jones's words are powerful and strong,
    prayerfully teaching what's good and what's wrong.
    What a wonderful way to praise the Lord,
    Jesus Christ, and the written word.

Dance Ministry

"I was created to make your praise glorious!"

Look at me! Just take a glance.
      Look at us! Watch us dance.
      Join the prayer we do for you
      and be a part of God's praise too.

It's not really me, it's God in me.
      His joy shines upon my face.
      He turns my awkwardness to grace
      and flows my arms and hands in ways
      that express His glorious praise.

His beat stirs my happy feet.
      His rhythm makes my body sway,
      and I become, through Him,
          a prayer.

**"Praise Him with the blast of the trumpet. Praise him with lyre and harp.
Praise him with timbrel and dance, praise him with strings and pipe.
Let everything that has breath praise the Lord! Alleluia."**

Psalm 150

The Coach's Story

Now we know what each of you
    believes in your heart is really true.
    It seems we heard each of you tell
    of a belief beyond what you hear, see or smell.

Is it our religion, then, that saves our souls?
    That shapes our lives? Sets our goals?

We all believe it's wrong to be cruel.
    We all believe in a golden rule.
    We all want respect. Then what we should do
    is respect what others believe to be true.

And let's just remember, once in a while,
    we each know the warmth of an honest smile.
    We each will sweat in the same hot sun
    and enjoy the same moon when our day is done.

When we wear our uniforms, we're so much the same.
    We're all intent on the soccer game.
    "I've been taught," someone cut in,
    "God made us the same, dressed in different skin."

Very well said! And if that is true,
    can't we let others believe what they do?

Ned's Dream

That night Ned had the strangest dream.
"Strange," he thought. "What could it mean?"
A place of worship. But why was he there
with so many people absorbed in prayer?

A choir was singing a song Ned knew,
    but the notes were wrong; they weren't really true.
    Ned sang out loud, as loud as he could.
    Maybe they'd hear him. He hoped they would.
    Then they'd know they were singing it wrong.
    Then they might start to sing the right song.

Others sang what they thought was right.
    They sang aloud, with all their might.
    Then children came and began to dance
    and jump and laugh and play and prance.

There were many ways to express the song.
    And each person thought the others were wrong.

Ned listened closely, and then he knew.
    The songs, though different, all rang true.
    "Life's that way," it occurred to Ned,
    thinking what his friends had said.

Even though we disagree,
    our lives can create great harmony.
    Each in our own and separate way,
    each together as one voice say:
    love of God, and all it might mean;
    love of neighbor, though hard it may seem.

Truth, respect and charity too,
    these are the things we all should do.
    And of all these things, one stands above:

To honestly, truly learn to love.

The Stories Behind the Stories

I could not have written this book had it not been for the generosity of so many who took me into their homes, their places of worship and their hearts, who were willing to speak openly with me about their beliefs and allow me to listen to their children tell me what they believed to be true. I was pleased that they welcomed the opportunity I gave them to share their religion with so many others in such a simple way.

What I tried to capture was the feelings of the children about their religion, not the dogma of their religion. Consider, for example, my interview with Gazal (pronounced "Guzzle"). I explained to her family that in order for me to write her story, I would have to pretend I was a Hindu child like Gazal. It would be easy for me to pretend to be a child, since I once was one, but I was never Hindu. They befriended me, welcomed me into their home on several occasions, took me to their temple, introduced me to Hindu food and Hindu prayer, and freely answered my questions. They did everything they could to enable me to be able to pretend to be Hindu. When I sat down to write Gazal's story, I could honestly pretend to feel as she felt.

It was an extraordinary experience for me, to join people as they prayed devoutly at their synagogue, their temple, their shrine, their church, their mosque, their sundance. With them I was able to feel I was in the presence of God, Yahweh, Brahman, the Creator or whatever you care to call Him or Her.

In the process of writing this book, I found myself growing from a sense of "religious tolerance" to a far richer and rewarding feeling of appreciation and respect for others' religious beliefs.

The stories that follow, what I call the stories behind the stories, are of necessity short, designed to give the reader just a glimpse of what and how I learned so much from so many good people. I thank them all for sharing, and I thank you for reading what they have told me.

The Coach

When I first began this book, I thought it would be helpful if I could find a mentor, someone who could help guide me through the religious and historical morass I was about to enter. I was looking for someone who had a religious background, who had a knowledge of religions other than their own, and who had the ability and willingness to be objective.

I had just about given up the search when I was introduced by a good friend, Joyce Tiley, to Pastor William E. Carpenter, D. Min., a Methodist minister in one of the northeast suburbs of Atlanta. Dr. Carpenter immediately was drawn to what I was trying to do. His knowledge and support throughout the project were of great help.

One of the struggles I was having was how to tee up the individual stories. Why would the children want to tell Ned about their religion? After several months, at one of our brainstorming sessions, Dr. Carpenter came up with the idea of the soccer game. The **Soccer Game** and the **Coach's Story** were both developed by him. I simply translated his thoughts into Ned-speak.

Christian – Lindsey Moon
age 9 years, from Duluth, Georgia

There were about ten children, aged nine to twelve, in our discussion group that Sunday morning at John's Creek Methodist Church. Dr. Carpenter had arranged for me to meet with the children as part of their Sunday school session in the hopes that I might get a story. The session did not go well. There were too many children, and the older children tended to dominate the conversation with comments that were not all that helpful. However, Lindsey Moon, a shy nine-year-old, who volunteered little but seemed to have so much more she wanted to say, intrigued me.

The following night Dr. Carpenter arranged for us to meet with Lindsey, her parents, Rusty and Mary Moon, and her fifteen-year-old brother, Nathan. He thought that the brother, who was very active in the church, might give me the story I was looking for.

Lindsey was happy to let her older brother do the talking. As Nathan told me how proud he was to be a Methodist, my mind drifted to the gathering the day before. We had been talking about Christ and love, and I remembered a comment Lindsey had made. I looked at Lindsey and said, "You told us yesterday that you no longer tell your mother at bedtime, 'I love you.' You say, 'I Christ you.' What did you mean by that?" Lindsey explained that the word love is used so many different ways that she wasn't sure what it meant. "But when you think of how Christ loves us, that's a special kind of love." We were all stunned, even her brother.

Lindsey did the talking from then on. She gave me her story, and it was a great one. Before my interview with Lindsey, I had no idea how I would accomplish what I wanted to do or even if I could. Hope and confidence came to me from a child younger than I would have thought possible. Now I was on a roll.

Hindu – Gazal Arora
age 9 years, from Duluth, Georgia

Mary Moon, Lindsey's mom, arranged for Dr. Carpenter and me to meet with four girls from Lindsey's Brownie troop: a Christian, a Jew, a Hindu and a Muslim. Each had mom or dad with them. What a wonderful opportunity, I thought. But again, I was to be disappointed.

I explained that the purpose of the meeting was to find beliefs that we have in common.

The discussion, led primarily by the adults, quickly turned to differences. Each time I tried to focus on what they had in common, it slipped back to differences. When you think of the great commonality of the major religions, why is it so hard for us to find it? Why must we seem to labor so intently on our differences?

Although the children were content to have their parent speak for them, Gazal was the exception. I was impressed by her warm and sincere feelings about her religion and the fact that her father proudly let her speak, willing to play a secondary role in the discussions. And yet, Gazal was an outsider, if you will. The three others could all trace their beliefs back to Abraham, Moses and the prophets. Gazal was Hindu. Her religion stems from an entirely different background.

It was not a surprise to Dr. Carpenter that I chose Gazal for my story on Hinduism.

The time I spent with Gazal and her family was a revelation for me. The Hindu traditions, rituals, mythology were so different from my own experience, I was amazed to find the same underlying message of love, the same respect for humanity and all life.

The time I spent with them, praying with them, in their temple, was a time spent in a holy place; a time, if you will, spent with not so much their God or my God, but with our God.

Jewish – Max Parker
age 12 years, from Naples, Florida

Max Parker and his nine-year-old sister, Sydney, live with their mother, Beverly Cahn, in Naples, Florida. I met them through their grandparents, Walter and Eddie Cahn, who are neighbors of Marie Leva, a dear friend of ours who lives on Marco Island, Florida. I was spending a week at her home working on this book. As a matter of fact, I've done most of the creative work for the Ned books at her home at a delightful spot among the mangroves looking out over a white sandy beach and the Gulf of Mexico.

Max and Sydney were happy and excited to talk about their religion. They were well versed in their Jewish traditions and customs. They adored their grandparents and always enjoyed their grandmother's special treats during the holidays.

They were easy to talk to; so I dared to ask Max an unfair question: "Do you believe the Jews are God's chosen people?" It was unfair, because I find most religious people you pose that question to would most assuredly say yes. That's why we feel so strongly about our religion. After all, God chose us!

Max's answer surprised me. He had the wisdom of ages in him. He just smiled and said, "That's what we're taught." Then he went on to say he believes that God chose the Jewish people to give the Ten Commandments and the Torah, and that's what I wrote.

Someone once told me, we only know what we've been taught.

Native American – Ricky Blackburn
age 15 years, from Riverton, Wyoming

In the Arapaho tradition, children are raised by their extended family. It is the role of the grandparents to educate the child and the role of the aunts and uncles to discipline the child. It is left to the parents to love the child.

I was introduced to Ricky Blackburn through his aunt, Marge Willow, whom I had met at a "Native Ways of Knowing" conference in Lander, Wyoming, just outside the Wind River Reservation.

Ricky Blackburn was unusual in that his two grandmothers were extraordinarily different.

His grandmother on his mother's side was a Shaman, a Healer, a Tribal spiritual leader well respected by the Arapaho people. It was through her that Ricky learned the ancient Arapaho way, the language, the dance, the customs.

His grandmother on his father's side was a very devout Catholic, influenced by the Jesuit Fathers and Sisters at Saint Stephens Mission. Ricky was raised to appreciate and love his Catholicism.

I was amazed at what I at first thought was the dichotomy of his religious beliefs. But the more I learned of the Arapaho and their Catholicism, the more I realized the dichotomy was only in my mind, not with the Arapaho.

There are many people throughout the world who, like the Arapaho, have taken the best of two or more cultures and crafted for themselves a life-ethic that works well. When you stop to think of it, it would be difficult today to find a religion that has not evolved from a combination of beliefs or a religion that has not been tempered in some manner by the needs of the times.

Mother Earth

Native Americans have a great respect for Mother Earth and all things created. This is a belief shared by many peoples throughout the world. The Arapaho express that respect and practice it in a way that most of us can learn from.

At Saint Stephens, Wyoming, there is a mission church established in 1884 by Jesuit missionaries for the Arapaho people on the Wind River Reservation. Covering the wall on the left of the altar in the chapel is a large painting called "The Creation." It was painted by Robert Blackburn, Ricky's cousin. I was so moved by this painting that I wanted to share it with you. I am grateful to the Jesuits and the Arapaho of Saint Stephens Mission for allowing me to do so.

According to a pamphlet available from the mission gift shop, " The Creation Mural depicts the earth as an Indian maiden, rising out of the power of the universe. As a representation of the earth, she holds in her hands the beginnings of life; the flora and fauna. Soaring behind the maiden is the image of an eagle, representing the spirit of life [The eagle is considered by the Arapaho to be the creature that can reach closest to the Creator and is sacred to them; they often ask the eagle to carry their prayers to the Creator]. By the Creator's will, the night was divided from the day as the earth began its orbit around the sun. This begins the seasons, which were seen as a representation of the cycles of life. The first day of spring [upper left] was the first day of the Indian New Year. The beginning of spring was much like the beginnings of life…new, young, and full. That gave way to growth and summer [upper right]. Then came adulthood, maturity and autumn [middle right]. Winter [middle left] became associated with old age and death."

Buddhist – Karma Lama
age 11 years, from New Paltz, New York

Karma is his given name. Lama is the family name given to Karma's grandparents when they fled Tibet by traveling a high and dangerous route over the Himalayas to the country of Nepal. They were on their way to India to join many other Tibetans who had fled Tibet when the occupying Chinese Communists outlawed their religion. In order to obtain a Nepalese visa to legally enter India, the Nepalese gave them the name Lama, as they did for many of the refugees from their region of Tibet, who traditionally had no last name.

I met Karma Lama, his sister Sherap, aged 6, and their mother at a Fire Puja, which is part of the weeklong preparations prior to Losar, the Tibetan New Year. A Puja is a prayer rite celebrated around a fire. I was given a few sprigs of evergreen. By watching others, I just followed suit, circled the fire and threw the sprigs into the flames. As I watched them burn, I could feel at peace as I imagined my troubles being consumed in the sacred fire. The purpose of the rite was to begin the New Year the following day with a clean heart. For Buddhists, it is a prayer for the expulsion of bad karma of all feeling beings throughout the world, not just themselves. It is a prayer for the world.

I remember sitting earlier that day and the day before in the Shrine listening to the monks pray, along with several devotees seated on the floor. All sat in Yoga fashion, with legs crossed. Hearing the low-pitched chanting of the monks, with each prayer ending in the sounding of a gong, the tinkling of hand bells and the low throb of ancient mountain horns, I felt in a sacred place and privileged to be joining in a solemn and ancient prayer for the world.

My meeting with Karma and Sherap was interesting because, by custom, the children were not instructed in Buddhism—not until they mature and choose it themselves as a way of life. So the children told me what they had observed, not so much what they were taught. They were excited to tell me of the visit to the town of Woodstock, New York, by the Dalai Lama, the spiritual leader of Tibet. They were particularly impressed by the story of the parrot; so I used that for Karma's story.

I was interested to learn what the children knew of their grandparents' ordeal in escaping from Tibet, but when I raised the issue, they had no idea what I meant. The mother did, and kindly made an excuse for them all to leave. I had taken the conversation into unwelcome territory.

A few hours later, at lunch, I discussed what had happened with one of the elder Tibetan men. He proceeded to teach me an important Buddhist belief. If we dwell on uncomfortable things that have happened, it serves no useful purpose and only hurts us, ourselves. If we harbor ill feelings toward those we believe have harmed us, they do not suffer from our ill feeling, we do.

Since then I have begun to realize what a powerful belief that is. It is a very important concept in the practice of Buddhism. I've been trying ever since to practice it, but for me it's tough; it's not part of my nature or part of my upbringing. But I find it does lead to a simpler life, with much less stress and anxiety. It makes it a lot easier to love.

The Buddhist Monk

Have you ever thought of what it might be like to be completely deprived of practicing your religion? Couldn't happen? It does; it has; it probably always will, somewhere, sometime.

While I was in the process of interviewing Karma, I met a young Buddhist monk at the Karma Triyana Dharmachakra Monastery in Woodstock. His name is Tashi Gawa, and he was born in 1971 in a mountain village in central Tibet near Lhasa, which was the capital when Tibet was an independent country. The magnificent old monastery in the village had not been used for over twenty years and was in great disrepair. The monks had long ago been scattered and were gone. Tashi Gawa was taught in a government school, where ethics and philosophy were taught from a little red book written by the Chinese Communist Leader Mao Tse-tung.

"Surely you were taught at home by your parents about their Buddhist beliefs," I said in ignorance. The truth of the matter was that his parents knew the danger. Had they talked about their Buddhist traditions, then surely he or one of his siblings would have made some off-hand remark to the wrong person, and his parents would be taken away.

Over time, things changed. The villagers began to rebuild the old monastery, and some of the monks returned. He found himself going to the monastery after school to hear the monks talk, out of curiosity at first. An old monk particularly impressed him. What that wise man had to say made the teachings of his little red book pale by comparison.

One day Tashi Gawa asked his parents if he could join the monks at the monastery. His parents refused. The native custom dictated that the oldest son should not become a monk because it was his role to see to the well-being of the family. But the more he learned from the monks, the more he wanted to join them. His parents finally agreed and were proud of him when, as a thirteen-year-old boy, he entered the monastery to become a Buddhist monk.

Muslim – Karam Salameh
age 9 years, from Somerset, Pennsylvania

I found the Muslim community in Southwestern Pennsylvania to be very friendly and helpful. They invited me to join them on a Saturday night for a community dinner at their small mosque. After dinner, I joined them in prayer. Then we sat around and as a group discussed my book and how they might help me.

Present that evening was Karam and his mother and dad and older brother. I was impressed with Karam and asked Fouad ElBayly, the Imam, their spiritual leader, if I might meet with Karam and his parents sometime in the privacy of their home.

The interview went well. Karam was happy to talk about what he believed. At dusk, the parents excused themselves for prayers and left Karam and me alone to talk further. Then they returned, and we finished the interview over Turkish coffee and Lebanese treats.

Karam's parents, Dr. Jawad and Shadia Salameh, are from Palestine and have been in America for over twenty years. I was saddened to learn how much their lives had changed since 9/11. The parents felt it more strongly than the children. They consider themselves to be American, and nothing that they have done or said or believe has changed that. And yet, on that day their lives changed. They felt those they had lived with and worked with for years suddenly considered them to be "non-American."

Horrible things have been done in the name of religion for centuries, and for centuries innocent people who have had nothing to do with those acts have suffered because of them. It amazes me how ill-meaning leaders have been and still are able to use religion for political purposes and for power. You'd think we would have learned by now.

Christian – Lillian Rowell
age 11 years, from West Chester, Pennsylvania

When we think of the major religions, we often fail to realize how many versions of each religion there really are. So many of us in America are Christian, and we are well aware of the many differences within that religion. But we often fail to realize that similar differences occur in other religions.

I chose to interview two Christian children of quite different backgrounds to help demonstrate that point.

I met Lillian Rowell and her mother through my friend Juan Baughn during Sunday school at St. Paul's Baptist Church in West Chester, Pennsylvania. Lillian spoke of the Sunday service as being "fun." I've never thought of it that way and was surprised. Religious services to me always seemed to be somewhat somber affairs. Even though they are often called a "celebration," they seemed to have a religious aura that precluded any thought of "fun."

You can imagine my surprise and joy when I did in fact experience the excitement and fun of her Baptist service. I have learned a great many things in this journey, but one of the most powerful was the experience of reverence being experienced through "fun." Yes, I learned having fun can be a beautiful and powerful form of prayer.

It was especially astonishing to me as I reflected on the oppression the black people I was praying with had endured in their recent heritage. What a joy it was to be with them, sharing with them, praying with them at that moment.

Lillian started dancing when she was four years old. Two years later, following her older sister's lead, she joined the Dance Ministry group at her church and loved it. She had found a special way to pray, using the talent she felt God had given her.

I was not familiar with Dance Ministry. Even with Lillian's attempts to explain it, I still did not understand what was different or special about this type of dance. Juan Baughn sent me a video showing Lillian and her group dancing. Her church had hosted about seven other dance ministries from other Christian (not Baptist) churches to join in a night of Dance Ministry. They called if, fittingly enough, "Joy Night." The phrase "I was created to make your praise glorious" was taken from one of the songs danced. Watching them, I knew; I knew how dance can be used as a beautiful and inviting form of prayer.

Ned's Dream

Dawn Audi was the hero of the book I wrote for the American Red Cross, *Ned and the Gift of Life, a lesson about blood*. Sadly, Dawn passed away a year ago after years of battling cancer. She left a husband, Dr. Fred Racke, and three small children: Karl, Bobbie, and Sophia.

Dr. Dawn, a pediatrician, kept a diary, and one of her last entries before she died was about a dream she had had. Her husband was kind enough to share that dream with me after her funeral. I felt her diary entry would be a perfect ending for my new book; so I rewrote Dawn's dream in Ned-speak and titled it "Ned's Dream," which appears on page 24. Every time I recall the story I think of her. I find it a provocative and beautiful ending to my book and a fond tribute to her. That's why I chose to dedicate this book to Dawn Audi.

Perhaps a fitting way to end this story is to quote one of my favorite people:

"Whatever you are, be a good one"
Abe Lincoln

Glossary

Abraham – Father of the Hebrew, Christian and the Muslim people.

Allah – The God of Islam.

Arapaho – Native American people formerly inhabiting what is now eastern Colorado and southeastern Wyoming.

Buddha – Siddhartha Gautama, 563? to 483? B.C. Indian Mystic who began preaching at the age of 35.

Buddhism – The teaching of Buddha that enlightenment obtained through right conduct, wisdom, and meditation releases one from desire and suffering.

Christ – The Messiah, as foretold by the Hebrew prophets.

Christianity – The religion derived from Jesus Christ, based on the Bible as sacred scripture and professed by Eastern, Roman Catholic, and Protestant bodies.

Christmas – A Christian feast commemorating the birth of Jesus.

Dalai Lama – The traditional governmental ruler and highest priest of the Tibetan Buddhism. The term refers to him as the ocean of compassion.

Eid al-Fitr – A feast that ends the Muslim feast of Ramadan.

God – The one Supreme Being, the creator and ruler of the universe.

Hanukkah – a holiday commemorating the rededication of the holy temple in Jerusalem after the Jews' 165 B.C.E. victory over the Hellenistic Syrians.

Hinduism – A diverse body of religion, philosophy, and culture native to India.

Holi – A popular Hindu spring festival observed in India.

Islam – the religious faith of Muslims including belief in Allah as the sole deity and in Mohammad as the chief and last prophet of Allah.

Jesus – A prophet whose life and teachings form the basis of Christianity. Christians believe Jesus to be the Son of God.

Judaism – A religion developed among the ancient Hebrews and characterized by belief in one transcendent God who has revealed himself to Abraham, Moses and the Hebrew prophets and by a religious life in accordance with Scriptures and rabbinic traditions.

Moses – Hebrew prophet and lawgiver who led the Israelites out of Egypt.

Mohammed – 570?–632 A.D. Arab prophet of Islam who began to preach as God's prophet of the true religion at the age of 40.

Ohm – In Hinduism and Buddhism, a sacred syllable uttered in affirmations and blessings and prayer.

Quran – The sacred text of Islam, considered by Muslims to contain the revelations of God to Mohammad.

Ramadan – The ninth month of the Islamic year observed as sacred with fasting practiced daily from dawn to sunset.

Ten Commandments – Ten rules of conduct given by God to Moses on Mount Sinai.

Torah – The body of wisdom and law contained in Jewish Scripture.

Yoga – A Hindu discipline aimed at training the consciousness for a state of perfect spiritual insight and tranquility and exercises practiced as part of that discipline.